Soft Spoken Words

Chelsea S. Thomas

Chapter One: The Lost One

Dear Sammie,

Where to start? Remember the night we went out with Jason and John? Something happened that darkened my soul. Words...words cannot begin to describe the emptiness I feel on the inside. The world that I imagined as a young child has been shattered in more ways than I can tell. My parents used to always tell me that the world was this amazing place to explore, and that it was waiting for me to take it by the horns and discover the beauty it provides. I find that funny now. Simply because they never told me that there is no light at the end of the tunnel. I remember the first time we met, you looked like a child at the candy store for the first time. The look of excitement and anxiety all in one was funny to watch. I would have never thought you would have become one of my dearest friends--more of a sister actually. Not because we came from two different worlds, but because you seemed more so in control of things than I was. The way you talked about your future and your plans could scare anyone who was indecisive about their future. I guess it was easier for me to pretend that I had all of the answers and knew what my future held, instead of admitting that I was confused and lost just like the next college student.

That night changed me, Sammie, and I have tried to deal with the pain. I feel like there is no one I can talk to....no one that will really listen without judgment. One can say that I could have had talked to you or my parents, but the truth is Sammie, I cannot bare to bother you or my parents with my troubles. You guys all look up to me, and I cannot bare the lectures, the stares, and the anger that comes with my secret. I have become filled with so much anger and hatred over these past months, and honestly I hate the person I have become. I HATE the way I look, feel, and smell. I HATE my hair, my smile, my body....I hate everything that I once loved about myself. I look in the mirror every day and I just fall apart. Sammie, I wish I could just tell you what is wrong with me, but you have been so busy lately, and you are doing so well in school, I don't want to distract you with my troubles. I am afraid Sammie. I am afraid of what I might to do myself--or even worse--what he might do. I have become consumed with so much bitterness and sadness lately, and the worst part is that I have been kicked out of school for not bringing my grades up after last semester. How can I tell my father who is lawyer and my mother who is a doctor that their only daughter was kicked out of school after her first semester? The looks my parents would give me would destroy me! They warned me of everything that happens at universities like this one, and I promised them I would be on my best behavior, and I wasn't.

Sammie...I am lost, and beyond damaged. I am to the point where there is no fixing me. .I feel like someone hit me with a car and came back and hit me with a hammer to make sure the job was done. I have...nothing...left. I am sorry Sammie. I will always cherish our friendship and the bond we have created during this short period of time. I love you chica!

Signed your southern gal, Erica

Chapter Two: First Day of What Determines What Type of Life We Will Live ~ College

It was Sunday, August 31, 2014, and it was the day I was going to move into the dorms at Harington University. I was moving 2 hours away from home, and a part of me was excited to finally be away from my parents and my younger sister Kate, but another part of me was nervous because I have never been that far away from home before. Crazy, an 18-year-old that has never been no more than 2 hours away from home, but this 18-year-old has never done a lot of things in her lifetime. I did not have or go to sleep overs like most teenage girls, and we barely took family vacations because my parents both had jobs, and money was tight growing up. The most damaging thing I had ever done was to forget to turn on my blinker at a red light when I was making a right turn. The only thing that happened in that situation was an impatient driver flicked me off because, they were unaware of the fact that I was slowing down to make a right turn. As I collected my things, and scanned my room to make sure I was not leaving anything behind, I discovered my teddy bear named Ted. My father gave Ted to me on my 12th birthday, and I decided to take him with me so that I was taking a piece of home with me to campus.

"Samantha! Are you ready to go honey?" My mother yelled. "Yes, I was just grabbing a few things." I took one more look around my room before leaving to head to school, and to my surprise I was ready to leave home and start this new journey in my life. "I am going to miss you Sam" said my younger sister Kate.

"Awe Kate, I am going to miss you too. You know I am only going to be 2 hours away, and I will be back for my breaks and stuff."

"Yeah I know but it is not the same, but I will just takeover your room to make up for you leaving" Kate says with a smile on her face. I ignored her and gave her a hug and a kiss on the forehead, and I told her goodbye. Kate and I are ten years apart and I knew she was going to miss me dearly, and I was going to miss her as well, but if there was anything I know about Kate, it was that no matter if I was at home or not, she would always go in my room without my permission and go through my things. It would normally irritate my soul but at this point in time, I did not mind because I knew me leaving was a hard thing for her.

The babysitter, Lauren, came over to the house to babysit Kate while my parents took me up to the school to help me settle in.

"Hey Sam, good luck with everything sweetie and be safe" Lauren says.

"Thank you. I will, and make sure Kate behaves herself." I give them both a hug and Kate another kiss on the forehead, and I get in the car with my parents. As we were leaving the driveway, I watched Kate wave goodbye, and as I was waving back, I realized that this was the beginning of something great. Although, I am extremely nervous about living on campus with strange people and living in a strange place that is not my home, I was ready to paint a new chapter in my life. There will no longer be Ms. Shy Samantha or the orchestra geek. No, not this time around, it was time to show people the real me, and not this false person I created to protect myself from getting rejected from my peers. Do not get me wrong, I am shy and I did play in the orchestra in high school, but there is more to me than that. I actually have been playing the violin for 8 years now. I first started playing the violin when I was 10 years old. My dad wanted me to play an instrument really bad when I was younger for some odd reason. He used to say music was a beautiful thing and that it should be an essential part of life. I could have quit in high school but I was really good with the violin, and it got me a full ride to Harington University, so I guess my dad knew what he was talking about.

Although I have a full ride to Harington University for playing the violin, I am majoring in Journalism and minoring in criminal justice. I always had a passion for writing and my obsession with law and order sealed the deal with that type of career I wanted after school. We finally pulled up to the university and the school was beautiful! The school colors were brown and gold and every building had those colors running through it. *Holy cow! This is huge.* "Pooh-Bear" my mother said.

"Yeah mom," Before my mother could respond to me, my father laughed and joked about how I might want to visit my classes before the start of classes so I didn't look like a total freshmen. I just rolled my eyes at my dad and told him that I wasn't going to look like a complete idiot on my first day of classes. *I hope not anyway. I think my dad has a point. I am making that my number one priority to find all of my classes.* My parents grabbed my things while I went to go check in and to get my keys to my dorm. I could not help but to be nervous because I was going to be living with strange people and the dorms were co-ed. *I have never been on a date before, let alone had my first kiss. Oh geesh I am such a dork.* I shook my thoughts as I got the front of the line. "Hello! How are you today?" The check in lady said. I was surprised by her enthusiasm and I felt compelled to respond with the same level of enthusiasm.

"HI! I AM DOING JUST GREAT!" I realized that I was shouting at the top of my lungs and I quickly looked away once I noticed how big her eyes had gotten.

"That is great, may I have your name please?" *Oh no, I came off as a jerk.*

"Yes, my name is Samantha Jones" I said with a smile and trying to get her back on my good side. "Okay Ms. Samantha, here are your keys. You are in Henry Hall dorms and your roommate is Erica Harris." I simply thanked the lady and grabbed my keys in a hurry.

Erica Harris. I hope she likes me. I did not understand why the school could not tell the students who they were going to room with, it was not like I was going to stalk the girl. I just wanted to get to know my new living buddy over the summer before we started school. "Are you ready Pooh-Bear?" my mother said. I told her yeah I was. My parents and I carried my things up to my dorm and I noticed my mother was becoming teary-eyed. *Oh boy! I do not want her to start crying because I am going to start crying.* I avoided making eye contact with her because I did not want the other people in the elevator to think that I was a big baby and that I never been away from home. Although, that was the truth, this was my chance to have a fresh start and to show people who the real Samantha was. As we entered into my room I noticed that the door was not locked and when we opened the door, there she was. Erica Harris. *OMG! She is gorgeous. Her hair has the perfect blonde and red high lights, with the perfect shade of brown hair. Her skin was the perfect brown and caramel mixed together. She has the perfect body! She looks like a coke bottle, not to big on the top and just right on the bottom.* I shook my head and caught myself before my mouth dropped open. My parents being the nice people that they are introduced themselves to Erica and her parents. *Her smile is even to die for! With her perfect white teeth, I pray to God that she is not like the girls I dealt with in High School.* "Hi, we are Samantha's parents, Charlie and Cindy" my father said as he went to shake Erica's parents hands.

"Nice to meet you" Erica's father said with a stern look. He barely smiled at my parents. Erica's parents were not too welcoming and they seemed pretty up tight. Our parents introduced us and they all bragged about our accomplishments in high school as if this was some type of competition on whose daughter is the best. I rolled my eyes and sat down on what looked like my bed. Erica came over to me and introduced herself and I couldn't find the words to say, so I just smiled. "Our parents are such dorks, aren't they?" she said.

"Yeah they really are and I am surprised my dad is acting that way. He is normally a really relaxed guy" I said.

"That's okay my father is very competitive and very intimidating. He is running to become judge in Texas, and he is the youngest black man to run to become the judge at that, so he tends to come off prune like" she said. *Oh wow! Room me with queen B, why don't yall?* I quickly shook my thoughts and told her that makes a lot of sense. I did not feel the need to go into detail about my parents since her dad seemed to have a more interesting career than my father. Do not get me wrong my parents both have wonderful jobs and my sister and I had everything we needed but Erica's dad was a big shot. I caught myself wondering what her mother did for a living, but I figured since our parents were in competition with one another already, that would be a question I could ask her at a later time.

As the time went on, our parents ended up laughing with one another and saying that they are glad that we were rooming with one another. Erica and I rolled our eyes at them and reminded them that we wanted to do stuff without them before it got too late. Our parents laughed and said they understood and told us that they wanted to wish us a goodbye. "I love you pooh-bear. You know you can always come home if you do not like it here" my mom said.

"I know mom. I will be fine, I promise." My mom began to cry and she hugged me very tight and I informed her that if she killed me before I could experience college from her tight hugging, I would haunt her for the rest of my life. She laughed and said sorry. My father isn't really good with letting go or letting me out of his sight, but surprisingly he told me that he would miss me and to chase my dreams. I found myself tearing up, but I realized Erica and her parents were also in the room, so I just hugged both of my parents really tight. I could not hear what Erica parents had said to her but, I did overhear her father telling her to behave herself and to not make him look bad. I felt kind of sorry for her because her parents are supposed to be having a sob moment with her, not telling her not to make them look bad. As a young adult entering college, how do you make your parents look bad? I really wanted to ask Mr. Harris how could Erica make her parents look bad but I was eavesdropping and that would've been rude, so I just continued to hug my parents. We said our goodbyes and our parents wished us the best and said they would see us later.

"I am so glad that is over! We can finally have some fun" Erica said. I informed her that I did not know what fun was and I have no idea what we should do next. She laughed at me and grabbed me by the hand and went to the elevator. *She doesn't seem so bad after all.* As we were heading to the elevator a few of the women that were on our floor came up to us and introduced themselves. I am not a talkative person, but Erica was and she had no problem introducing herself and me to other people. The way she talked to people, you would think that she had a career in public speaking or something. Erica dominated the entire conversation and she did in a way that you wouldn't get intimidated by her. She allowed people to talk and she kept eye contact the entire conversation. I caught myself wondering if she was some kind of spy or something because I have never seen someone my age take control of a conversation like she did. Anyways we got onto the elevator and she asked me to tell her about myself. *What kind of question is that? Is this like a friendship interview or something?* "Um I have a younger sister named Kate and she is my world! I play the violin and that is how I have a full ride to this school. Um, my parents are married and have been my entire" before I could finish the rest of my sentence Erica interrupted me. "No silly. Tell me about what you like to do, but I did enjoy speaking and meeting your parents today. They seem like great people." I did not know how to tell her that there is not much to know about me. I never had a sleepover, never been kissed or dated a guy, I do not have any friends, and I hide in my writing. I just told her that she will find out all about me by hanging out with me. She just smiled and grabbed my hand as we were leaving the elevator.

We pulled our schedules and found our classes and majority of Erica's classes were on the opposite side of the school from mine because she was majoring in criminal justice with a minor in law. It was no surprise that she wanted to become a lawyer because her father was a lawyer and he seemed like he had her entire life picked out for her. Hanging out with Erica was extremely fun and I realized that I probably prejudged her before I even had a conversation with her. We laughed and met a lot of new and cool people. I found myself thinking that maybe after all I will finally be able to be myself and I possibly found a person that could become a good friend. We went into the school's cafeteria to see what our major organizations were talking about. They had a lot to say and I had an idea of what kind of organization I wanted to join and I knew that I wanted to become a member of our newspaper, and build as many connections as I possibly could. As the night came to an end, Erica had managed to find out where the party was at for later that night and told me that we were going, and that she would find me something really cute to wear. I did not like the fact that she assumed that I did not have anything to wear, as if I am some kind of dork, even if that was the truth. Erica noticed that I had rolled my eyes at her and she quickly apologized for what she said. I told her it was okay, and that I did not mind. We went back to our dorm and she helped me pick out an outfit, and I laid it on my bed. I tried to lay down to take a quick nap but, Erica kept talking to me about how much fun we were going to have this semester and how she was excited that I was her roommate. I just sat on my bed and smiled at her and thought to myself about how I am going to have a new start.

Chapter 3: The Ultimate Blow-Out Party

It was 10:00pm and Erica was bugging me to hurry up and get dressed. I was excited to go to my first college party…well my first party but, I was nervous because I didn't know what to expect at events like these. "Sammie! Is it okay if I call you that?" said Erica. *I never had a nick name besides pooh-bear or honey, and that was from my mother. The names my mother called me weren't really nicknames to be honest.* I realized I was in deep thought and I quickly answered Erica before she came out of the bathroom.

"I don't mind" I said.

"Okay, cool! Come here for a second and sit down in this chair" Erica demanded. She was so bossy but, it wasn't a rude bossy, it was a sweet bossy. I quickly went into the bathroom and she looked really hot! Her hair was curled, she had on a pink shirt that showed off her piercings and tattoos, she had on tight blue jeans, and pink lip gloss with the eye shadow to match. When she smiled it lit up the entire room, I could not help but to think about how God had made such a beautiful creature. Erica grabbed my arm and sat me down in the chair.

"What are you doing Erica?" I said in a low pitched voice.

"I'm going to do your makeup and hair. I picked out another outfit for you to wear instead of the other one we picked out earlier. We are going to be the hottest women at this party" Erica said. I couldn't disagree with her because I so desperately wanted to be one of the prettiest girls at the party. It took her about forty minutes to finish my hair and makeup, and when she handed me the mirror I could not believe the person I was looking at in the mirror. I started crying and I hugged Erica really tight and thanked her for her master work. She ensured me that she didn't do much but bring out the woman that was hiding behind her bangs.

Erica pulled out her smart phone and took a selfie of us and captioned it, "my new bestie." I found myself smiling and thinking that it was awesome to have met someone like her and I couldn't wait to see what our college days would bring us. Erica and I walked to the elevator and I could not get her to be quiet about the party. I just laughed and smiled, and once the elevator doors opened she grabbed my hand again. I got into Erica's car and I could not believe that an 18-year-old had a brand new Bentley. Erica must had noticed my reaction because she said, "it's cute isn't it?" I just told her yeah it is. The party was off campus and it was about 15 minutes from the school. We pulled up to the party and got out of the car, and every guy eyes were on Erica. I felt out of place and I wanted to go back to the dorms but Erica came over to me and told me it was going to be okay. I thought it would be the perfect time to tell her that I was dork and that I have never been to a party or been kissed by a boy. "That's okay Sammie, I will be right by your side and I promise you will have the best night of your life. As for your first kiss" before she finished her sentence, she grabbed my face and kissed me. *What the hell? I DO NOT LIKE GIRLS! I DON'T KNOW HOW I GAVE OFF THAT IMPRESSION. I know I have never been kissed but I wanted my first kiss to be with a guy not a girl. I hope I won't lose a good friend over me not being gay.* When I came back to reality, all I heard was guys cheering us on and clapping. "THAT'S HOW YOU GET A PARTY STARTED! TOO HOT CHICKS MAKING OUT! WHOOT WHOOT" *They think I'm hot. Awesome!* When I opened my eyes, Erica just winked at me and grabbed my arm and headed into the party.

I couldn't think of anything else but that kiss Erica gave me. I did not know how to tell her that I was not into girls and that I hoped it wouldn't ruin our new developed friendship. She looked over to me and whispered in my ear, "I don't like girls either. I just did that to break the ice so you wouldn't feel so nervous." *You didn't have to use your tongue if that was the case.* I was puzzled because it was as if she was inside my mind. Two guys came into our direction and they had drinks in their hands. *Oh boy! Here we go. Keep calm and be cool.*

"Hey beautiful and her gorgeous friend! That was a nice performance you guys put on out front" said one guy.

"You liked?" Erica said while batting her eyes.

"I did. What are your names? My name is Jason and this is Matthew and this is our party."

"My name is Erica and this is Sammie, and this is really a nice party you guys have going on."

"We try our best. Listen, how about yall come with us over to the other side. They have some games going on over there" Jason said.

"Sure, but are those drinks in your hands for us?" Erica said.

"Yes they are" Jason said. They handed us the drinks and they grabbed our hands but, Erica pulled away and said that they can lead us to the other area and she continued to hold my hand. I appreciated the fact that she did not let go of my hand and that she stayed by my side the entire night. When we got to the other side, they were playing a game I never heard of, and it looked fun until Erica volunteered us to play the game.

"Erica, what are you doing?" I said in a low voice.

"Don't worry you'll be fine. I will be right here with you, I promise" Erica said. That relieved some tension off of me until they informed me that it would be drinking involved. *Holy cow!*

A guy named John yelled the rules out, "IF YOU NEVER DONE SOMETHING THAT IS MENTIONED YOU HAVE TO TAKE A SHOT! IF YOU REFUSE TO TAKE A SHOT YOU HAVE TO STRIP TO YOUR UNDERWEAR AND RUN AROUND OUTSIDE NAKED!" *YOU HAVE TO BE FLIPPIN KIDDING ME!* Erica grabbed my arm and started yelling like a crazy person with excitement.

We were all in a circle and the first person went. *Suck it up Sam. This is your chance to have fun.* "I never kissed a girl" one girl said. *Thank god for Erica!* It was a few people that took a shot. "I never had sex outside of my parents' house" one girl said. *Welp, here it goes.* I felt like I was the only person that drunk to that and after my first shot, the night had officially begun. All I can remember after like the fifth one, I was on the dance floor with Erica and the two guys we met earlier. We were dancing and everyone around me was having a good time. I felt like I was the life of the party, and I hope I really was and not one of those drunk people who look like idiots. I lost track of time and when I recalled the time I was back at my dorm in my bed. I am assuming that Erica helped me to the car and into my bed, and I felt kind of bad because I know a drunken person can be heavy to carry.

"Erica! I am glad I met you. I am glad we are roommates. You...You know you are...are so awesome! Although...that kiss...the kiss was odd...I like guys not girls you know" couldn't help what was coming out of my mouth, it was like I had no filter.

"Yeah I know you like guys Sammie. You were making out with that guy, Pete" Erica said while laughing.

"I like Pete! What kind of name is Pete?" I giggled and the next thing I knew I was fast asleep. I remember hearing Erica telling me to get some sleep and that she knows we are going to be really good friends.

Chapter 4: Picking Dorkey Organizations to Get Involved In

I woke up the next morning to a note, a red Gatorade, a bottle of water, some wheat toast, and two aspirins. *Was my mother here this morning? Does she know about last night? Oh lord!* "Hey Sammie! Eat up so we can go check out some of these organizations" said Erica. *She is so awesome! I just love her.* All I could manage to say was okay. I still felt like crap so I just threw on some jeans and a tank top, and sunglasses to cover up the bags under my eyes with my Detroit hat and my chucks to match. Erica was so loud and it gave me a migraine, so I hurried up and took the aspirin and ate my toast. She kept going on and on about the different types of organizations, the guys from last night, and how this year was going to be so much fun. I just nodded my head and rolled my eyes behind my sunglasses, and smiled as if I was not annoyed by her constant talking. She asked me if I was ready to go and I simply told her yeah. I think she could sense that I had an attitude but I did not care, I just wanted her to talk less until the medicine kicked in.

We went into the recreation center where they were holding the information about the different types of organizations to get involved in. There must of had been some type of "organization God" because when I laid eyes on the journalism stand and after quickly glancing through the board about what the organization has to offer, I immediately broke out of my hanger over coma and pulled Erica into the direction of the journalism stand. When I looked back at her she was smiling and was just going with the flow. We sat in on one of the 30 minute sessions to listen to what the organization was all about. "The journalism organization is all about helping you become a better writer. You can apply for an internship with us, editorial position, a writer position, or a photography position with this organization. And if you do not like the sound of that, if you join this organization your membership fees will cover the cost for you to become a member of the National Black Journalist Association, and that will connect you with the best resources on how to become a successful black journalist" said the president of the organization. *I think I just died and went to heaven! This is awesome!! Now I can finally start chasing my dreams of becoming a writer, and I can build connections with people who know how to survive in this world full of other journalists.* "Close your mouth why don't ya?" laughed Erica. I rolled my eyes at her and I was kind of annoyed by her reaction because she does not know my story, and she does not know what I have been through my entire life. I am not sure she knows what it is like to struggle or to not have nice things and to get bullied at school because your family could not afford the designer clothes. "I did not mean to make you upset Sammie, it was a joke. I know you are excited about this and I know you will have the GPA at the end of the semester to get into the organization, so relax and have fun," said Erica. I just simply rolled my eyes and turned my head back in the direction the guy was talking and finished listening to the perks of being a part of this organization.

After the guy finished talking I told Erica that we should go to the criminal justice club to see what they were all about, and she said okay. As we were sitting and listening to the president of the CRJ club talk about all of the perks, I looked over at Erica to see if she was just as excited as I was when I learning about my organization. She did not look very happy. In fact, she did not seem to be interested in the organization at all. *Her father is a lawyer in Texas, so I am pretty sure that all she has to do is obtain her degree and the rest is done for her. Must be nice.* I shook my thoughts and tried to help Erica become engaged in the conversation and with the members but she did not seem like her normal self. When the president of the organization came over to speak with Erica, her entire mood changed. She became alert and she was even smiling as if she was listening the entire time. They exchanged conversation between one another and I did not care to listen. I did not like how Erica was pretending to be interested in something and I did not like how she could switch her mood within one second, it made me question if she was pretending to be my friend. I could not help but to think about how she made smart comments about my clothes and how she was so nice. *No one is that nice.* I quickly shook my thoughts once again and told Erica I was going to go for a walk and she did not seem to care about where I was going.

As I was walking around outside my thoughts started to take over and I could not help but to feel fooled by Erica. *What if she was pretending to be my friend? What if she feels sorry for me? Well I don't care! I feel sorry for someone who doesn't have parents who care about them! If she doesn't want to be my friend for real, then I do not care. I did not come to college to make friends... stop it Samantha! Maybe she has to be friendly with him, maybe his parents knows her father. Just get to the bottom of it before you start making assumptions.* When I turned around I had seen Erica walking in my direction and waving. I waved back because I did not want to be rude. "You want to grab some lunch?" said Erica. I told her sure why not. We walked over to the cafeteria and it was this awkward silence and I was surprised that Erica was not talking as much as she had. We got burgers to eat for lunch and found a booth to eat in. "Are you okay, Erica?" I asked. She just continued to eat her burger as if I had said nothing to her. I could not help but to get annoyed by her ignoring me and I did not know what to do to get her to speak to me, so I did the first thing that came to mind. "OUCH!" yelled Erica. "Why did you just kick me?" she said. "Because you ignored me when I asked you a question" I said with an annoyed tone in my voice. "Sammie, I am sorry that I ignored you but sometimes people have more important things going on in their lives to deal with instead of all of your questions! Sometimes I just like to sit in silence" she said. *Oh really? Since when does Erica Harris have nothing to say?* I could not come up with anything to say but okay.

She saw the look in my eyes and she quickly apologized for snapping on me and not answering my question. She then went on to explain why she was so tense and why she acted the way she acted at the criminal justice club organizational meeting. *I swear this girl can read my mind. How does she know that I knew she was acting weird at the meeting?* "Why were you acting anti-social at first then social when that guy came over?" I asked. "Sammie, it is a lot of things you do not know about my family and I," Erica said as she held her head down facing her food. I have never seen Erica like this before and I know we have only known each other for a short period of time, but we have spent a lot of time together and I have never seen her behave this way. I simply told her that she could tell me anything and I would not judge her. She looked at me and smiled and it was as if she had all of the answers she needed in order for her to trust me.

"Sammie, as you know my father is the first black man to officially run for the judge position in Texas, and he has had a very successful career as a lawyer. Growing up I had everything I could every want and more but I never had my parents. My mother is a very successful doctor and that is accomplishment within itself because, she is a black woman and a doctor. My parents are both very successful and they put so much pressure on me to be just like them. I always got straight A's and if I ever received a B my parents would ground me. People always think that we are the perfect family and that is not the case. I can count on my hand how many family vacations we have been on and how many woman-to-woman talks my mother and I had. The only thing my parents every talked to me about is success and how hard it is for black people to become successful. 'Leave the boys alone and keep your head in the books and everything else will be taken care of for you' my dad always said. I don't know what it feels like to have parents that care about what you want and to actually spend time with you. That is why I kind of got down when we were at the event today. I was excited at first but then I thought about how important it was for me to become president of the criminal justice organization and to develop connections with the director and the president of the organization. I just got extremely nervous and I just wanted to sit in silence for a while" said Erica.

I was lost for words, and here I thought she had the perfect life because her parents were better off than mine. I never appreciated my parents for their love and affection more than I did at this very moment. Growing up I may have never had what I wanted but I had everything I needed and we always spent time together as a family. My family and I are very close and I could not understand how Erica's family could not be close. I felt like the lucky one after hearing Erica and why she was behaving that way, and I could not help but to feel bad for her. I stood up and I went to the other side of the table and gave Erica a hug. "Every family has their issues and no one is perfect. I am more than sure that your parents love and care about you, they just want the best for you. Being black in America is a very hard thing and when you have parents who know what it takes to become successful in a world with all of the odds stacked against them is a blessing. Your parents just want the best for you, and that is great and all but at some point in your life you have to start living for yourself. You are an amazing girl and I know you are going to be great in life no matter what you decide to be. You only get one life to live, sweetie, so make it count" I said. She smiled and gave me a huge hug and thanked me for my words of encouragement.

"Now that is over let's go have some fun!" Erica said. I was shocked at how she could switch her emotions on and off but I was happy that she was back to her happy self. She grabbed my hand as usual and we headed back to our dorm.

Chapter 5: Double Date

It was a Saturday night and Erica and I were watching movies in our pajamas and eating ice cream when her cell phone rung. "You know I am still jealous that you have the newest IPhone and I have this old android" I said while laughing.

"Your phone is cute Sammie! Don't be jealous girly" Erica giggled. When I looked up from my ice cream bowl, Erica was jumping up and down like a little school girl. I asked her why she was acting like a school girl and she told me to guess.

"Your father said we can use his cabin for our winter break?" I said.

"Umm no! Remember that guy from that party we went to a while ago?" she said.

"Oh lord! Do not remind me about that crazy night," I said as I giggled.

"That guy Jason just texted me asking me did we want to go on a double date with him and his friend Johnathan" Erica said with a big smile on her face.

"I hope you told him no to the double date" I said.

"No! I told him yes and that we would come over to his apartment in about an hour" she said.

"Why would you do that? I don't want to embarrass myself again Erica!" I said while laughing.

"Look woman! We are going and we are going to have a fabulous time. So get up and get ready" Erica said as she was pulling me up from my bed.

"Okay but you have to give me something to wear" I said.

"No problem! I have the perfect outfit" she said.

We got dressed and as always Erica looked flawless and she had on the perfect outfit that showed off her curves. She picked me out this pretty outfit and surprisingly I had curves as well. I laughed at myself in the mirror and Erica came over and took a selfie and later posted it on Instagram. We got in Erica's car and we went over to Jason's apartment and while in the car Erica was extremely happy. I have never seen her this happy before, so it was safe to assume she really liked this guy. I just sat back and enjoyed the breeze and listened to Beyoncé on the radio. As we arrived to the apartment, I was becoming nervous. Erica ensured me that I was going to have a good time tonight, and to let my panties out of a bunch. I really did not know exactly what she meant by that, but I just laughed and figured she meant for me to be myself. As we got out of the car Jason came over to the car and gave Erica a hug and a kiss on the cheek. He told her she looked gorgeous as always and that he missed her. I could not help but to wonder if they had hung out before and she never told me or were they texting and she kept it a secret because to my knowledge they only met and hung out once, and that was at the party. I just stood there as they talked to one another and Jason apologized for his rude behavior and he called Johnathan out.

"John, this is the beautiful Samantha I have been telling you about, and Samantha this is my handsome bud John" Jason said. I just smiled and told Johnathan hi.

"He never mentioned that you looked this beautiful before. I mean he said you were cute but my… my you are flawless. And please call me John," he said.

"Why thank you, John" I said while blushing.

Erica and Jason were heading into the apartment and they told us to come on. I thought it was so cute how they were all holding hands and acting all kiddy like. John was not so bad himself. He was really cute! He had that athletic body with the right-sized muscles, his clothes fitted him, and he had the perfect white smile. He also had the perfect shade of caramel skin and curly hair, and I could not help but to wonder why this beautiful guy was interested in me. I think he could tell I was nervous because he grabbed my hand and we walked into the apartment. *OMG! HE IS HOLDNG MY HAND. Okay be calm and don't mess this up! He is really hot.* I shook my thoughts really quickly and made sure I did not trip over my feet as we were walking into the apartment. The guys took us to their living room and we were all talking and Jason ordered pizza and put in a movie called "Love Don't Cost A Thing." I was shocked that he picked that movie because Jason was white and I did not know white people watched movies like that. Maybe that shows a lot about me, that I am also guilty of putting white people in boxes like they do us.

Thirty minutes later the pizza arrived and we were all eating pizza, drinking, and laughing. I was careful to not get drunk this time because I really liked John and I did not want him to think I was a complete dork. As the laughs started to dim out John put his around me and pulled me close to him. *OMG! WHAT DO I DO, WHAT DO I DO?!?* I shook my head and just told myself to play it cool and not to look like a complete dork. I glanced over to where Erica and Jason were and their tongues were locked. I have never seen two people kiss like the way they did besides on the chick flicks I watch on television. I felt so inexperienced and I had no idea what was going through John's head. *He probably thinks that I am a loser and he is never going to want to hang out with me again.* I think John could tell that I was inside of my head because he just smiled and grabbed my hand. It was like he was secretly trying to reassure me that he knew I was inexperienced, as if he had a heads up prior to us coming over. I kind of stated to frown at the thought but quickly stopped myself, and Erica and Jason told us they were going to go somewhere private. "Are you going to be okay down here by yourself?" Erica asked me. I could not tell her not to leave me because I did not want to be left with a guy I just met but I did not want to look like a complete dork so I said it was okay. I found myself wondering what they were going to do and when I finally dawned on me what they were going to do, my mouth dropped open. John looked at me and asked me if I was okay, and I told him that I could not believe the movie was over and that it was my favorite movie. *Good answer!* He laughed and insured me that we could put in another movie and I said okay. Although, my parents gave me the talk about sex and how to protect myself, it never really crossed my mind until now. I guess I never thought that I would ever lose my virginity because I never had a boyfriend before and I guess since I was going to be hanging with Erica now it might come up more often.

Erica and Jason were gone and it was just me and John by ourselves. It was that awkward silence with the movie playing and I wished Erica was in the living room with me so she could break the silence. The visual thoughts about Erica and Jason having sex were constantly going through my mind and I felt nervous and compelled to be doing the same thing with John.

"How did you and Erica meet?" John asked.

"Um we are roommates. How did you and Jason meet?" I asked.

"We met our freshmen year as roommates as well and he was really cool so we just kicked it and kept each other as roommates, and now that is my bro" he said while laughing.

"So what is your status? And what is your major" I said.

"I am a senior and I major in business with a minor in communication" he said.

"That is awesome!" I said. *I hope that wasn't too loud.*

"Yeah it is. My parents both own their own businesses and my father has a part time job as a professor teaching people how to run their own business. But enough about me, I know you are a freshmen, but what is your major?" he said.

Geesh does everyone parents have a cooler job than my parents. "My major is journalism with a minor in criminal justice. My goal is to become a crime reporter one day" I said while blushing.

"That's wonderful! We need more honest black journalist" he said.

I think I just fell in love! I just smiled back at him and gazed into his hazel eyes. I swear this guy could melt a glacier with his smile. After the awkward questioning faze we began talking and surprisingly I wasn't nervous anymore. He was not a bad guy and he really seemed to be into me, but then again that could all just be an act. My mother told me not to trust guys with pretty eyes because they know how to lie their booties off. I laughed at the thought and

John asked me what was so funny and I just told him I was really nervous to be down here with him by myself, but I am not nervous anymore.

"Why were you nervous to be down here with me by yourself?" he asked while laughing.

Okay try not to sound like a complete dork. "Because I have never been alone with a guy before" I said. *Well done dork!*

He pulled away from me and looked as if he was trying to see if I was lying and I guess when he realized I was not lying he started laughing. I got offended and rolled my eyes and he quickly apologized.

"I am sorry. It is just that you don't meet too many women who say that" he said.

"Well I am not like most women, I am very different" I said with an attitude.

"I know. I can tell and I like different," he said.

I tried not to smile but I could not help it, he was so charming and cute. Either he was trying to talk his way into my pants or he really meant what he said, either way it felt good to have a male's attention. We were laughing and watching movies and getting to know one another. I was no longer thinking about Erica and Jason having sex or whatever they were doing, I was just concerned about getting to know John. John told me he really liked me and that he wanted my number so we could go out on a date. *A date! Oh yeah!!* I shook my thoughts and grabbed his phone and put my number in it and called my phone. *That YouTube video came in handy about how to be cute when giving a guy your number!* I giggled and stored his number in my phone once I got it through my text messages. "Is it okay if I kiss you?" John said. I was shocked that someone would ask another person if they could kiss them, but I must admit it was really cute. I told him yeah he could kiss me and as our lips locked I could feel my soul come out of my body and spin around and enter back into my body. His lips were so soft and I never knew that people could move their tongue around someone else's in a manner where it feels that they their tongue is on the inside of you. I felt an unusual feeling at the pit of my stomach and I thought that he was going to kick it into the next gear and start unbuttoning my pants, but he whispered that we weren't going to have sex tonight. I was lost for words and I did not know what to do or say, I have never met someone like him. How can he be so in control of this situation and how can he say "we aren't going to have sex tonight," like dude? The way I am feeling it could most definitely happen tonight. *Say something sexy.* When I found the words, I told him if he was only so lucky. He giggled and pulled me closer to him, it was to the point where I was sitting on top of his lap.

As we were sitting on the couch kissing and laughing, Erica came down stairs in a hurry. I jumped off of Jason's lap and fixed my shirt and he put a pillow over his lap. *Oh yeah! He wanted me.* I did not know much about sex but I knew what bonners looked like because of the one incident this guy had in my eighth grade class. Anyway, we asked her what was wrong and before she could say anything, Jason came down the stairs. The way Erica looked at him could break a little girl's heart. She looked at him as if she was disgusted by him, and when I asked her what happened again she just shouted she was ready to go and ran out of the door.

"What the hell did you do to her?" I said to Jason. *Hell? Since when did you curse? But you used the right word. HELL!*

"Nothing! She just freaked out because I said I was not going to call her tonight" he said.

I could not tell if he was telling the truth or not but I told him he better call her and that if he hurt her I will kill him. He laughed and apologized for being a guy and for messing up John and I's bonding time, and he promised he would call her tonight. I grabbed my things and shook my head at Jason and told John to text or call me later, and he told me he would and he gave me a kiss goodnight. I do not know how I could be this happy when my best friend is miserable right now, but I cannot help it. John is awesome! I walked out to the car and Erica looked like she was crying but when I asked her what was wrong she just said nothing. We got in the car and we drove back to the dorm in silence, and I must admit I have never seen someone so spaced out before. Erica looked like she received some horrible news about a loved one and she did not want to talk about it. This was unusual behavior for her, but no matter what I tried she would not tell me what was bothering her. We got back to the dorm and Erica walked straight to the dorm and got right in the bed and she put a pillow over her head. My phone distracted me from what was going on with Erica and to my surprise it was John. I started smiling and put on my pajamas and lay in my bed.

Do you know what happened between Jason and Erica? –Sam

Nope. I asked him what happened and why she was acting that way, and he just said she was upset about him telling her that he wasn't going to text her tonight. –John

That is a very odd reason for her to react that way. That does not seem like Erica. –Sam

You might be right, but that is not my business. My business at the moment is getting to know this beautiful woman that I spent the evening with. –John

Maybe you are right. What do you want to know? ☺ –Sam

John and I texted the entire night and I felt all types of goose bumps and butterflies in my stomach. Before putting my headphones in my ear I overheard Erica in the bathroom crying, and I so badly wanted to go in there and demand that she tells me what is wrong with her, but maybe John was right. Maybe it is none of our business, and figured she would tell me when she was ready to tell me what was bothering her. So I wrote a sticky note and put back in my headphones and continued texting John.

I love you! You're an amazing woman and any guy would be lucky to have you. Whenever you are ready to talk I am here for you. Xoxo your Sammie ☺

Chapter 6: Withdrawn

It was a Saturday night in November and Sammie and I went over to Jason's apartment to watch movies with his friend John. I really like Jason and he makes me feel so special, something my father never really did. I have always had guys pay attention to me and try to get inside my pants but I promised myself I would save myself for that special guy. I am not looking for a husband, just someone who truly understands me and who is not all about getting in my pants. The first night I met Jason, he was so cute and really laid back. I have always had a thing for white alethic guys, and I can promise you that I might end up marrying one, one of these days lol. Any who, we immediately clicked at the party and we hung out a few times after the party, but we texted a lot. Besides for Sammie, Jason is the only person that I feel close to in a short period of time. My father is always telling me how not to trust people and that everyone has motives but I just think that is my dad being the grouch that he is. I felt closer to Sammie and Jason more so then I have felt to my own parents in years, and maybe it is because of my parent's jobs, Idk. So it was Saturday night and we went over to Jason's house to hang out and Jason and I went somewhere private. I was kind of nervous but not really. I figured tonight would be the night I could possibly lose my virginity to Jason if he played his cards right. We were kissing and he was unbuttoning my *shirt and pants, and he got up to make sure the door was locked. He reached under his bed and pulled out a huge toy chest and the look in his eyes when he looked at me scared me. I just laughed it off and I started kissing him again...*

■ ■

Over the next few weeks I have been hanging out with John and hanging out with the people who are a part of the journalism club. Every time I asked Erica to do something with me she would say that she did not feel like it and curl back into her bed and pull the covers over her head. I kept asking her if Jason called her and if that was why she was acting this way, and she just ignored me. It got to a point where her parents started calling me and asking me how she was and why she wasn't answering her phone. I lied to her parents and told them that she was really busy with school and that she would call them when she got some spare time, and they would simply say "okay, that is my girl." I did not understand how parents could be okay with not speaking to their daughter for weeks and taking some strangers word for her wellbeing. I know if that was my parents they would have drove up to the school and made sure I was alive. I tried my hardest to put the Erica drama out of my mind and focus on school and my developing relationship with John, but the promise we made to one another kept coming to my mind. *We promise that this is our year! It is us against the world. No matter what we promise to always be here for one another.* I just did not know how to be there for someone who did not want you to be there for them. I just gave Erica her space and focused on the things that wanted me around.

One day, the founder of the criminal justice club approached me and asked me why Erica has not been coming to their meetings and he noticed that her grades were slipping. I thought to myself for a brief moment how someone could access that kind of information before responding to his question. I told him that I had no idea that her grades were slipping and that she was not showing up to the meetings. I ensured him that she really wanted to be a part of the club and that she was struggling in some classes, but she is getting some help. He looked at me with a firm look to see if I was lying and he said "very well, tell her to email me," and I told him okay. I did not like how Erica was turning me into a liar, and I felt very upset with her and how she was refusing to tell me what was wrong with her. If I was supposed to be her best friend then best friends are supposed to tell each other what is going on. I marched back to the dorms and demanded that she tell me why she hasn't been going to her meetings and why her grades had been slipping. *I am not sure if I was supposed to tell her that part.* The look she gave me melted my heart. She looked like she has been crying for weeks and as if she hasn't eaten anything. The bags under her eyes were so dark and her cheeks were red and puffy. Her hair even looked like it hasn't been combed in months and she smelled really bad. She did not answer my question and when I tried to get her up into the shower she flipped out on me. "JUST LEAVE ME THE HELL ALONE SAMANTHA!" I pushed her back down and told her that I hated the person she has become and she is my best friend and I am trying to help her, and I walked out. I tried my hardest not to cry, but I was filled with so much anger and it was directed towards Erica. I felt so bad for yelling at her but she will not tell me what is going on with her and I am becoming someone that I do not like. I ran down stairs and I bumped into John.

"Hey there beautiful" he said.

"Hi" I said.

"What is wrong with you?" he said.

"Nothing" I said in a snobby voice.

"Those tears don't look like nothing. Come here" he said. He grabbed my waist and pulled me to nearest bench and refused to let me go until I told him what was bothering him. How could I refuse his puppy dog look with his pretty eyes? I simply told him what was going on with Erica and she has been acting different ever since the night we all hung out. I told him that she is turning me into a liar and I do not like that.

"I am glad you do not like to lie..." he said as he giggled.

"I am being serious John, something is wrong with my friend." I hit him for laughing and told him if Jason hurt her I would kill him. He ensured me that Jason did not hurt her and that we would all get together tonight and maybe that would cheer her up. I gave him a huge hug and he kissed me, and I told him that I was going to tell Erica the great news and to see him later.

▪▪

It happened again! The darkness came inside of me and this time it brought friends. I refused and told it that I did not want to but it just hit me and held me down. The darkness had something over me and no one could ever know and I hated what it has done to me. I do not feel like myself and I hate myself. Again and again and again the darkness entered me. No one can save me!

▪▪

I ran up the stairs and into my dorm and shouted at the top of my lungs. "I KNOW WHY YOU ARE UPSET!" Erica looked at me as if she was surprised and relieved, but when I mentioned going out with Jason and John she became angry.

"We are all going out to dinner" I said.

"I'm not going" she said.

"Why not Erica?" John said Jason was sorry for not calling you. If looks could kill, I would have had just died with the look Erica just gave me.

"I AM NOT GOING ANYWHERE WITH HIM! GO BY YOUR DAMNSELF" she shouted.

"YOU KNOW WHAT ERICA? I HAVE BEEN NOTHING BUT NICE TO YOU BUT I AM TIRED OF YOUR BULL! YOU ARE A MISERABLE PERSON AND YOU ARE BRINGING ME DOWN. I CANT DO IT ANYMORE!" I yelled.

"What do you mean?" Erica said. If I knew I was going to regret my next words I would of never had said them.

"I CANNOT KEEP LOOKING AFTER YOU ANYMORE. YOU NEED SERIOUS HELP. I'M DONE CARING!" I yelled. I had so much built up anger towards Erica that I could not help the words that came out of my mouth. She mumbled fine, and rolled back over and went to sleep. I felt so bad about how I reacted. It is obvious that she needs me, and that she is suffering from a broken heart and all I care about is my feelings but, I am exhausted with school and everything else and I do not have time to deal with someone who doesn't want to be bothered with me. I turned around and walked out of our room and turned the lights off as I walked out.

Chapter 7-Winter Break

It was the last week of classes and everyone was freaked out about finals. I have been studying very hard to end my first semester with a 3.8 GPA so I could become a member of the journalism club next semester. I have been going to all of their meetings and I have been volunteering and connecting with all of the right people in the organization to show them that I am serious about becoming a part of this organization. On top of me being involved with the organization and school, I have been hanging out a lot with John. I guess it is safe to assume we are dating and that I really like him. He is a really smart and hardworking guy, and he makes me feel really good about myself. With everything going on in my life, I must admit after the argument Erica and I got into, I have not seen much of her lately besides from when I go back to my dorm to go to sleep. Apart of me felt bad about how we do not talk as much as we used to but, she just seems to want to be by herself, so I just left her alone. We have small conversations about her plans for the break and how school is going with her, and she just gives me brief and quick answers. Although, Erica and I do not hang out or talk as much as we used to, I still consider her my best friend and surprisingly she tells me that she misses how things used to be. Whenever I ask her or tell her that we can go back to how things used to be and that I still love her and that I am here for her, she just says things will never go back to being the same and walk away.

I was in my dorm and I was on the phone with my parents when Erica walked in the room. "Hey honey! Are you ready to come home for break?" my mother said.

"Hey mom, umm I'm not so sure I'm ready to go home…I really enjoy my freedom" I said while laughing.

"You can still have your freedom pooh-bear, and your sister and father misses you very much…I miss my girl very much" my mother said in a soft toned voice.

"I know mom, I miss you guys as well, can you guys come pick me up Friday after my last class?" I said.

"Yeah…what time is that? Maybe we will bring Kate with us and we can all grab dinner and a movie after" my mother said.

"My last class is at 3pm, and that would be great! I really miss my munchkin," I said while laughing.

My mother ended our conversation by telling me she loved me and see me tomorrow, and I told her that I loved her as well and hung up the phone. When I got off of the phone, Erica was looking out of the window and she was looking like a sad puppy. I really did not want to bother her with my questions but, I felt compelled to ask her what she was going to be doing over break. No surprise to me, she told me that she was going to stay on campus over the break because she did not want to go home. Although, I expected her to say that, I was surprised because what parents do not want to see their child that they have not seen in three months? I asked her why she did not want to go home to see her parents and she just looked out the window and told me because they are too busy for her due to her father's campaign. As a child, I know that must hurt that your parents are too busy to miss you and to spend time with you, and as her best friend I could not let her stay on campus by herself. She was going to be spending Christmas by herself, and I already let her spend thanksgiving by herself, and my conscience could not let her spend another holiday alone.

"Erica, do you…no Erica you are coming to stay with me this break and we are going to have some fun! You deserve it," I said in a demanding voice.

"Sammie, I--" I finished her sentence before she could tell me no.

"Yes, you can go, and you are going. My parents do not mind if you stay with us over the break, they would love to have you over. So pack your bags, we are leaving tomorrow after class" I said.

"O…okay" she said in a low toned voice.

I was surprised my demanding tone worked. Normally she would get an attitude and tell me to leave her alone. But to my surprise she looked relieved that someone wanted to spend the holiday with her and I felt that I fulfilled my duty as a best friend. I told her that I was going to meet up with John and asked if she wanted to come with me, and she just stared at me. So I repeated myself and she shook her head no and turned back around and continued to look out of the window and started writing in her journal. I really wanted to know what she was looking at and what she was writing in her journal, so I asked.

"Hey Erica, what are you over there writing and thinking about?" I said.

"Not to be rude but, it is none of your concern. My journal entries are private and I do not discuss them with anyone, but I am looking forward to spending winter break with you and your family" she said.

"Okay, no offense taken. I understand, and I am too! It has been a while since we hung out together," I said.

She just smiled and continued to write and look out the window. I normally would have had gotten upset at her smart remarks, but I have not seen her smile or say she was happy about something for a while, so I just took it and accepted it for what it was. I could not help but wonder if I would get my friend back over break, and if she would open up about what happened between her and Jason that night. If she decided to, I promised myself that I would not judge her and that I would listen to what she said and tell her how much guys are jerks. *Well not my guy, he is amazing.* I shook my head and told her I would see her later and she said okay.

I was wearing high waist blue jeans with an orange tank top with gold accessories to match, and I had on brown chucks on. I will admit that Erica taught me how to color coordinate my clothes with my accessories and she taught me how to put on a little makeup. My hair is shoulder length and I have jet-black hair, and today I decided to wear my hair straight. I had on tannish eye shadow and mascara with mac clear coconut lip-gloss. *I look really pretty today!* Erica's skin color is lighter than mine and growing up I used to believe that dark-skinned girls were not pretty because that is what I heard my entire life, but meeting Erica has taught me to love the skin I have, and that I am beautiful inside and out. Anyways, I was excited to see John before leaving to go home for the break. He is really funny and fun to be around and I would be lying if I said that I did not want to be his girlfriend, but I cannot help but to think that being his girlfriend comes with other things. The female drama, him possibly not wanting to settle down with a freshman, and of course sex! Sex in relationships is very important and I am not sure that I am ready to have sex with a guy that I just met a couple months ago, I barely know the guy. I am just going to try not to bring up our relationship to him, and just go with the flow, besides he graduates next semester so I might not have to even bring it up.

When John and I met up, he gave me a hug and a kiss, and he told me that I looked really beautiful today. *Boy does he know how to make a gal feel special.* I just smiled at him and thanked him for the compliment, and told him he didn't look bad his self. We walked over to the cafeteria and we were holding hands and talking and laughing all the way over there. I noticed when we got to the cafeteria and picked our seats a few girls were looking at me and pointing, and I kept checking my small mirror to see if I had something on my face because I could not understand why they were looking at me. Then it dawned on me that I was with John, and maybe they were upset that I was having lunch with him. He came back to the table with our food with this bright smile on his face and when he noticed that my face was frowned up he asked me what was wrong with me. I told him that his groupies were looking at me and that they were upset with him. He rolled his eyes at me and sat down and told me not to worry about them, and that he was here with me so I should focus on that and not the girls who aren't on a date with him. His arrogance and his demanding tone irritated me and it made me think about Erica, and how she would never let a guy say that to her. So I took a deep breath and said the first thing that came to mind.

"What are we?" I said. *Oh no! Here we go, by beautiful Jonathan.* He looked puzzled as he thought that I already knew that we were just hanging and nothing more. I started to regret the words that had come out of mouth, and I kicked myself for getting upset about the girls pointing at me. Maybe I should have had listened to John and just enjoyed our time and tuned them out, but as a human being and a woman I need to know where this was going. Were we just hanging, were we just friends, was he just being nice so he could eventually get inside my pants and then leave me alone like Jason left Erica alone? Are we together, or are we just dating? I needed to know and it was driving me crazy just sitting here while he collected his thoughts.

"Well" I said. *I like the new me. You go girl!!*

"I do not understand what you are asking me," he said.

I don't see how someone who is as smart as him could be this clueless to a question like this. "Are we together, dating, are you just trying to get in pants, are we just hanging out? Is that better for you?" I said in an irritated voice.

He started laughing, and it irritated the hell out of me! "I don't see what is so funny, I am being serious!"

"Don't you think that is an elementary…high school kind of question to ask?" he said.

I could not believe how stubborn he was being and it made me think that we were just two friends who were hanging out and he was trying to get in my pants after all. John had seen the look on my face, and immediately stopped laughing and started talking again. "I mean the only reason you asked me that question was because of those girls, but if it would make you feel better we are dating. I want us to date one another and see if this could develop into something more." As he was speaking my heart jumped out of my chest and I felt like a schoolgirl all over again.

"Okay, that sounds good to me. Sorry for acting that way" I said while smiling.

"It is okay, I understand where you were coming from. But just know I think you are beautiful, you are a wonderful person, and I really enjoy talking and hanging out with you. Of course with me being a man I want to have sex with you but I am willing to wait until you are ready" he said.

I was speechless and I just started smiling and I got up and sat in his lap and kissed him. I was shocked by my actions because the old me would have had never did that, I would of just sat there and starred at him. *I really do love the person I am becoming.* I thought to myself. I was just sitting in his lap and we were laughing and talking about our plans over break, and I told him Erica was coming home with me. He asked me how she was doing and I told him she is doing better I believe and he said that was good. He walked me back to my dorm so I could pack my things to go home tomorrow, and he told me that he was going to miss me. I felt so special and I told him that I was going to miss him as well and that I would be back before he knew it. We kissed goodbye and he gave me a big hug. I decided not to tell my parents about John because I did not want them going into protective mode and asking to meet him. We are not official yet but we are dating and I wanted us to get to know one another better before he met my parents. I walked back to my dorm with my head in the clouds and to my surprise Erica had all of her bags packed and she was watching television. My mouth dropped and I just starred at her and she smiled back and offered me some cookies and cream ice cream. I grabbed my blanket, a bowel, a spoon, and sat on her bed with her and watched movies. I did not ask her how she was feeling, and I did not tell her about my amazing afternoon with John, I just laid on her bed in silence and enjoyed her presence. It felt good to have my friend back, even if it was for a split second.

It's 3pm and it was Friday, and my parents were downstairs waiting for us to come down. Erica was smiling and she was in a good mood, and I did not know what to think but I decided to enjoy her being happy for a change. My mother was waiting by the car with open arms and when I hugged her, my little sister Kate opened the door and jumped on me. I was laughing and it felt so good to see my family, and I did not realize how much I missed them until now. My father was putting our bags into the car and he gave me a tight hug and told me that he missed me and I told him the same. Erica was just standing outside of the car smiling and she looked as if she was analyzing my family and I. I decided to introduce her to my sister, Kate, and Erica and Kate clicked immediately and I was glad they did. My mother gave Erica a hug and told her how happy she was that she was spending the break with us and that we were going to have lots of fun. Erica smiled and told my mother that she couldn't wait, and we all got into the car. We went out to dinner that night and Erica was not her usual self. She normally dominated conversations and was always talkative but today she was full of life and she looked as if she just wanted to fit in with us normal folks. We were all laughing and Erica and I were telling my parents about our first semester experience. My mother asked about Erica's parents and Erica just said that they were busy at work and with her father's campaign, and that they wanted her to enjoy her break. My mother nodded and said that it was their loss and our gain and she continued telling some more of her corny jokes.

Later that night Erica and I were in my room and we were watching movies with Kate. I told Kate that I was proud of her not destroying my room and that since she was on her best behavior I was going to bring her to the school for sibling's day. She was so excited that she gave me a huge hug and said she was going to tell mommy and daddy the good news. Erica and I laughed and Erica told me that I was lucky to have such a beautiful family. I told her she has a nice family as well, but she just ignored what I said and told me that her parents are busy with their jobs to notice her. I felt really bad and it was that moment that I decided to ask her what was going on with her at school. She told me she was just going through something and things are going to get better. Erica looked as if she wanted to tell me something but was afraid to, and I did not want to make her upset because she was finally happy, so I just took her word for it. Instead, I gave her a hug and told her how much she meant to me and that she is officially stuck with me for the rest of her life. She laughed and told me that I was the sister she always wanted and that she loved me and she was glad she met me. We started watching another movie and we were laughing at the people in the movie. It was that night we had made a promise to one another and we promised to remain sisters no matter what and to always be there for one another. During the entire break my parents had things planned for us to do and reconnected our friendship and I was glad to finally have my friend back. We went to the movies, we had family dinners, we volunteered at various organizations, and I showed Erica my neighborhood. My father even let her drive his car and I was shocked because he is so over bearing whenever I would drive his car, but I guess that is because I am his daughter. Our break was only one month but we enjoyed every last bit of it and Erica had a blast!

Chapter 8- The Lost Soul

My parents dropped us off at school and it was a bittersweet feeling because I had a lot of fun when I was home, but at the same time I was ready to come back to school. Of course I was ready to see my guy, but I also missed all of the new people I have met through the organization. I kissed my parents goodbye and they gave Erica a hug goodbye and they told her that she was welcomed to come over anytime. I thought Erica would go back to being her gloomy self when we arrived back to the school but she didn't. She wasn't the same Erica I met, she has changed and I did not know why, but I liked it. We loaded our things up and when my parents drove off I had seen John heading in my direction. I was so excited to see him and I did not know that he would show up this soon after I texted him. I guess he missed me just as much as I missed him.

"Sammie! Areee…you…" as Erica was asking me if I was ready to go upstairs she noticed that Jason was with John. The look on her face was heart breaking. It looked as if she lost someone dear to her. She just stood there in shock, and I asked her what was wrong and I insured her that I did not know John was bringing Jason.

"I can't…I can't…I…" is all Erica kept saying. Before I could gather my words to tell John that I would come to him, the guys were both in our faces.

"Hey Sam! How are you? Erica! I called you over break. Why didn't you return my phone calls? Jason said.

When I looked at Erica's face and at Jason's face I could not understand why they were acting so strange. Erica did not answer Jason, and she just walked away in a hasty manner. I told John to bring our things up and I yelled at Jason to leave Erica the hell alone and to never speak to me again. I ran after her and grabbed her before she got to the elevator, and I apologized for John bringing Jason with him. I told her that I had no idea that John was going to come see me this fast and that she should not forget her promise she made to herself. She snatched her arm away from me and told me to leave her the hell alone and walked away. If it wasn't for the crowd we attracted by our yelling I probably would have had started crying. I could not believe that Erica would react and yell at me the way she did. I felt so embarrassed and angry that I took my frustrations out on John.

"WHY THE HELL DID YOU BRING HIM HERE WITH YOU!?" I yelled.

"I did not know that it was that intense between them two, and I did not invite him, he invited himself," John said.

"DO YOU KNOW WHAT HE DID TO HER? WHY IS SHE ACTING THIS WAY! YOU BETTER GO BACK TO YOUR APARTMENT JASON. NOBODY WANTS YOU HERE!" I continued to yell. I felt bad for taking my anger out on John but I was so upset that Erica was upset, and I needed answers.

"You know what, I do not get into other people's business and neither should you. I can see you have an attitude so I will catch you later before I say something I may regret" John said in an irritated voice. Before I could say anything he was calling out Jason's name for him to wait up for him. Once again I was left looking stupid in front of people because of Erica. I just grabbed our bags and headed back to our dorm.

The next day I got up and I noticed Erica had been writing in her journal and when I tried to grab it she woke up.

"What are you doing?" Erica said.

"I need to know what is going on with you. You are acting strange, you are depressed, you are writing in your journal and you have changed. As your best friend I deserve to know what is going on with you" I said in demanding voice.

"I…" before Erica could finish her sentence my phone went off. I looked at my phone and put it back down.

"Well…" I said.

"Nothing…I…umm...nothing" she said. The look in her eyes looked as if she was disappointed and it broke my heart into a million pieces to see her this way. I had no words left, no strength left. I just walked to the bathroom and left Erica sitting up on her bed. I put on my sweat pants and hoodie, and put my hair in a ponytail. I brushed my teeth and put on my gym shoes and went for a walk to clear my mind. I just left Erica sitting in the bed with her thoughts, and if I knew what I know now, I would of have never done that. I don't know how someone can be so happy one minute and then down the next! She was just so happy over break. *Why won't she talk to me! I don't know what to do anymore. I cannot have a repeat of last semester. She is my best friend and we just made a promise to one another. WHAT THE HELL HAPPENED BETWEEN THEM!* As I snapped back to reality, I realized I was outside walking in the rain and a couple of hours have passed by. Whenever it rains my arms get itchy so I ran back to the dorms to avoid my arms becoming really itchy.

I dried my feet at the door and I opened the door. It was really quiet in the room, no music was playing and that was unusual for Erica. I cut on the lights and when I went over to Erica's bed my heart stopped. The room was spinning and everything went black, I heard someone screaming and I could not figure out who was screaming and for what. When I seen our RA burst in my room I realized that girl that was screaming was me.

"WHAT IS GOING ON IN HERE?" she yelled. I could not find the words so I just pointed.

"Oh my god! Get back" she said as she was calling the police. Tears were coming down my face so fast and I thought I was sleeping in my bed having a terrible nightmare, but my dream was a reality. The paramedics were checking her pulse and doing multiple procedures on her and she just stood still.

"WAKE UP ERICA! PLEASE I NEED YOU!" I could not stop the words from coming out of my mouth.

"Call it," they said.

"CALL WHAT?" I said.

"8:00pm" they said.

"WAIT! STOP PLEASE…8:00 WHAT?" I said.

"She is g…o…n…e…ma'am. I am sorry for your lost. She overdosed on pills," they said. As the words came out of their mouths I fell to the floor. I cannot believe it.

"SHE…S…H...E…NO…N…O...GONE! NO, NO, PLEASE GOD NO!" I cried. The RA was holding me as I was crying and the hallway was filled with people and people were crying and in misbelief. I started yelling and shouting telling the paramedics to bring her back to me but they kept apologizing and put her on a transportable bed and covered her up. As they were taking her body out, I just kept picturing her in my mind. I kept replaying everything over and over again, and I kept saying she was just here, and that it was my fault.

She looked so cold. Her spirit had left her body and I was too late. I let my friend die and she is gone. If I would have had come back sooner, she would still be here. The police came into our room and they were asking me questions but I had no answers. "Was she depressed?" "Depressed, no…I don't think so… she was down a lot. "Did she have a boyfriend?" "Boyfriend? No…" "Did she have trouble in school?" "No…I don't know…maybe." It was question after question and I just felt angry and confused and to be honest I just wanted to wake up from this horrible nightmare. After they were done with their questions, they escorted me out and told me that they are going to get down to the bottom of this. The RA told me that I could sleep in her room until tomorrow morning, and that they would figure out where I was going to be staying next. I felt like someone had ripped out and stolen my heart and set it on fire, and I could not understand why this was happening to me. I did not understand how she could be gone and we just seen each other. I blamed myself for leaving her alone and for not being a good friend like I promised. My phone kept ringing and I let it ring until it died, and I cried all night. I could not stop thinking about how she felt, and that my beautiful southern gal was gone. I was no longer going to see her smile anymore, or hear her laugh, or even hug her. She was gone and there was nothing I could do about it. I could not close my eyes because that moment kept replaying in my mind, so I just cried until I could not cry anymore. *She's gone…She's gone…this can't be real…Erica please…I'm sorry…I love…you…no…no.*

Those weeks following her death were hell! I could not breathe…I could not speak…I felt so lost and confused. It was as if I lost of piece of myself, and I did not know how to get it back. I could not understand why she would do that to herself and why she wouldn't talk to me about what was going on with her. She knew that I cared deeply about her and that I would have done anything for her, so I just found myself confused most days. I ignored everyone that was calling my phone except for my parents. My mother did not know what to say to me, so we just sat in silence over the phone most nights. I appreciated the silence my mother and I shared over the phone because I was so tired of talking about what happened and not knowing why she did it. I had numerous of nightmares about that night and I often woke up in the middle of the night crying and yelling. It got so bad that the dean of the school approved my parents' request for me having my own room. My father would often ask me if I wanted to come home but I felt so close to her spirit at school. We shared so many memories at the school, and I did not want to leave what we shared at the school to go home. So my father eventually stopped asking me and he would just check in on me from time to time.

I can recall her funeral and her parent's reactions when they came to the school to pick up her things. They looked as if they were in disbelief and if it was not for her mother jumping into Erica's casket at the funeral I would of have thought it did not bother them. The funeral was packed with a lot of people, and I knew immediately that Erica left behind a lot of people who cared about her. I questioned myself repeatedly on how she could be so selfish and how she could ever believe that people did not care about her? I found myself hating her for leaving me and shutting me out all of those months and I became angry and sad. I felt guilty about the way I was feeling and I knew I had no right to feel that way, but I could not help it. I can remember as her body was being put into the ground I felt a part of me leave. I have known her for a short period of time but it felt like a lifetime. She was the Batman to my Robin, the peanut butter to my jelly, and you cannot have one without the other. She left me all alone and she never even said goodbye, and as her parents said their goodbyes, I just starred at her grave as they were covering it with dirt. I could not say goodbye because saying goodbye would mean she was really gone, and at the time I did not want her to be gone. I just wanted to remember all of the times we shared and the promises we made to one another, and saying goodbye to that was not an option to me. I must have had lost track of time because my mother grabbed my hand and told me that everyone was getting in their car to leave. It was that moment that I fell to ground and started yelling and crying and shouting at her grave. "WHY ERICA?...WHY…WHY…" my mother started crying and telling me that sometimes people are going through things that they cannot share with others and how life tends to have mysterious things that happen with no explanation, and how she wish she could take my pain away. I just cried and my mother held me, and we just sat on the ground.

Chapter 9- The Lies She Told

It has been about two months since Erica's death and my grades dropped and I stopped participating in the journalism club. I just wanted to be left alone and I did not care about anything else. Whenever my parents asked me how school was going, I would lie and tell them it was going great. I could not tell them that I got accepted to the journalism club but I turned it down because I was depressed. I could not even find the words to tell them that my full ride scholarship was in jeopardy because my grades had slipped. They would make me come home and to take time away from school and I did not want to do that because I did not want to leave the place where I felt the closes to Erica. I even stopped talking to John. He would call and text me and say how sorry he was for my loss but I did not want to hear what he had to say, I just wanted to be alone.

One evening when I was laying in the bed and when I got up to use the bathroom I tripped over some boxes. *Damn it!* When I went to go stack them back up I realized it was Erica's boxes. Her parents gave me something's of hers and they told me that she would've wanted me to have them. I opened the first box and went through it, and it was just some of her accessories and scarfs that she always would wear, and I immediately started crying and laughing at the memories of her. When I opened the second box I found some of her favorite books and her journal. I started to have flashback of when she used to write in her journal and how she would get upset whenever I asked her what she was writing about. I wiped my tears and went over to my desk and started to read her journal. She wrote about the things we did and how much I meant to her and by reading her entries about me I started crying again.

Dear Journal, Sammie is amazing! If I ever had a sister I would hope that my sister would be exactly like her. She is the sweetest person I know and I feel like she knows more about me than the people who have been in my life longer. She doesn't know this though, but she is really my only friend. I have more associates than friends and the girls at my high school was always jealous of me or I did not have any time to make friends because I was either shadowing my father at court or at home reading my favorite books.

She went on and on about her life and how she wanted a fresh start at school. As I was reading I found journal entries about Jason. *Finally! I can find out what happened between them.* She talked about how they hung out a few times after the party we went to and how much they texted, and how much she liked him.

Dear Journal, Jason is awesome! I really like him. He listens to me more than my father and to my surprise we are both from Texas and his father is running against my father for the seat of becoming the new judge. I know I probably shouldn't talk to him and if my father found out he would be so mad, but I don't care and neither does he. We connected on a level that I have never connected with a guy before and I really hope this could turn into something serious.

I found myself thinking that they seemed to have a lot in common and that was odd that they were from the same place. I guess Harrington University is the school for future lawyers. I could not put her journal down because I felt so close to her again and I wanted to know what happened to her. My stomach was upset with me because it was starving but I could not put the journal down, so I just drunk a banana smoothie and continued reading. She talked about how much she liked him and how she was excited for our double date. Erica also mentioned that she was a virgin and how this night could be the night that Jason and her do the deed. The voice on the inside of my mind shouted *A VIRGIN! NO FLIPPIN WAY.* I really couldn't put her journal down now, and it was as if I was watching a really good movie and I couldn't cut it off.

Dear Journal, It was a Saturday night in November and Sammie and I went over to Jason's apartment to watch movies with his friend John. I really like Jason and he makes me feel so special, something my father never really did. I have always had guys pay attention to me and try to get inside my pants but I promised myself I would save myself for that special guy. I am not looking for a husband just someone who truly understands me and who is not all about getting in my pants. The first night I met Jason, he was so cute and really laid back. I have always had a thing for white alethic guys, and I can promise you that I might end up marrying one, one of these days lol. Any who, we immediately clicked at the party and we hung out a few times after the party, but we texted a lot. Besides for Sammie, Jason is the only person that I feel close to in a short period of time. My father is always telling me how not to trust people and that everyone has motives but I just think that is my dad being the grouch that he is. I felt closer to Sammie and Jason more so then I have felt to my own parents in years, and maybe it is because of my parent's jobs, Idk. So it was Saturday night and we went over to Jason's house to hang out and Jason and I went somewhere private. I was kind of nervous but not really. I figured tonight would be the night I could possibly lose my virginity to Jason if he played his cards right. We were kissing and he was un-buttoning my shirt and pants, and he got up to make sure the door was locked. He reached under his bed and pulled out a huge toy chest and the look in his eyes when he looked at me scared me. I just laughed it off and I started kissing him again. He told me that he wanted to tie me up with the ropes he had in his toy chest and blind fold me. I was a virgin and I never imagined my first time being tied up, and to be honest that was just weird. I laughed and told him no and that I did not want to. Jason pushed me off of him and when I asked him what was the matter he smacked me. I could not believe that someone so gentle could turn so violent in a split second. I tried to get up and head for the door but he grabbed my arm and threw me on the bed. I started crying and told him that I wanted to leave and that he was scaring me and he laughed and called me a bitch. "You bitches think that you call the shots and that you can play with a guy and tell him no!" I told him that I did not say no I just said no to getting tied up, but he did not want to hear what I had to say. The only thing Jason heard was no, and if I knew that he was into weird things I would of have never went somewhere private with him.

I begged for him to let me go and I would not tell anyone about what happened in the room and that it would be our secret, but he would not listen. He started pulling the rope out of his toy chest, and whenever I tried to go for the door he would grab me and throw me on the bed and hit me. He grabbed my face and kissed me, and I tried to refuse but he was so strong! "Are you going to be a good girl" he asked. I started yelling and telling him that my father would have his ass locked up so fast and he would be spending the rest of his life behind bars. That made him very angry and he punched me in the face so hard that my nose started bleeding. "Tell your father what? How much of a black whore you are! Have you forgotten about your little show you put on at that party? Did you forget about all of the pictures you sent me? I haven't and I have them all ready to send to your precious father. Bitch, do you know who my father is? I will have your ass out on the street so fast begging for help. I will ruin your life and your fathers campaign bitch!" he yelled. I so badly hoped someone would hear him yelling or that Sammie would come looking for me, but no one came. I kept crying and I believe it excited him. How can someone be this cruel? How could I be so stupid? I begged and begged for Jason to let me go and that he did not have to do this but he just grabbed my arms and told me if I refused he would show everyone my pictures and videos from the party. My father words kept going through my mind about how I was to behave and not to make him look bad.

I tried to reason with Jason and tell him that I didn't want to have sex with him anymore but he just laughed and tied the ropes around my arms tighter. He asked me again if I was going to behave or if he was going to have to send my father and the media the videos and pictures, I told him I would behave and he said good. He had my arms and legs tied and I was facing him. He told me that we were going to have a lot of fun and that I would enjoy it. I just cried and told him that he did not have to do this. I have never been so scared in my life and I have never wanted someone to come rescue me, but no one should up, it was Jason and I. He grabbed my face and he forced himself into me, and whenever I closed my eyes he would tell me to open them and if I closed them it would be worse then what it is. Again and again and again and again he rammed himself into me. I just blacked out and went to my happy place because I did not want to be in my body anymore. He licked my body all over and he put different objects inside of me and the look in his eyes was evil. I felt like this pain would never end, and it seemed to go on for hours. Once he was finished he penetrated inside of the condom and flushed it down the toilet before untying me. I cried and I felt extremely sore, humiliated, scared, and angry.

He threw a rag and towel at me and told me to get cleaned up. When I tried to close the door he told me to leave it open and to get cleaned up in front of him. I did not argue with him and as I was cleaning myself up I seen him staring at me through the mirror. I became angry and yelled at him, "you got what you wanted". He came up behind me and pulled my hair and told me that I was his and that he owned me, and that he could and would have me whenever he wanted to. I started crying and he wiped my tears and kissed me and told me that this is what I wanted. I told him it wasn't and he reassured me it was, and that if I told anyone about this he would ruin my life and my father's career. I just wanted to get out of there! When I came down stairs I seen Sammie and John kissing and when Sammie asked me what was wrong I wanted to tell her. Jason came down the stairs right after me and I just ran out of the apartment. No one could see the bruises because I covered them up with makeup and no one noticed the limp in my walk because they were too busy with their own lives. Everyone probably thought I deserved what I got anyway! I cried myself to sleep that night.

The anger and guilt I felt consumed my entire body. I felt my entire body become hot and tears started rolling down my face. I could not ready anymore of her journal entry, but my mind forced me to continue to read her journal entries. Night after night Jason tormented me in some kind of way. I just wanted to die! I so badly wish I could tell someone...maybe Sammie. I actually tried to tell her a couple of times but she was always so busy with school and John. I just did not want to bother her with my troubles. Jason raped me again but this time he brought people with him. They each took their turns with me and when I refused and tried to fight back he would hit me harder. He told me that he owned me and that whenever he calls me I better make myself available to him and whoever else he wanted. I asked him several times why he was doing this to me and I thought he cared about me, and he told me that he did care about me, and that I was his sex slave. I became angry with Sammie and my parents because they did not care about me! They were only concerned with their own lives and although a part of me believed that wasn't true, I couldn't help how I felt.

I punched the head board of my desk and I felt like I failed Erica, and it is no wonder why she did not want to talk to me. I was so concerned with my life and what I felt, and I ignored the signs of her pain. I continued reading the journal and I had to control my anger because I so badly wanted to go kill Jason.

Dear Journal, Winter break was amazing! I finally felt free. Jason told me not to leave campus for winter break but I told him my father was forcing me to come home. I lied to him of course because I spent my break with Sammie and her family but I did not want to run into Jason at home. I loved spending time with Sammie and her family, they made me feel so special and for a split second I forgot about all of my troubles. Jason texted and threatened me the entire break but I did not care. This time with Sammie and her family allowed me to get my confidence back, and it felt so good to hang out with my best friend again. Boy how I missed her and her laugh. We made a promise to one another over break, and I was going to tell Sammie what has been going on with me, but I decided to leave the past in the past and move forward. I decided that I was going to get professional help and let Jason do whatever he was going to do... I no longer cared.

My heart felt a little pressure after reading that passage and I felt a little happy that she had found her happy place again, but I was confused as to why she took her life, so I continued reading.

Dear Journal, I was prepared to go visit the dean and ask for a second chance and to explain to them that I was dealing with a personal issue but I am prepared to work ten times harder to bring my grades up if they let me stay at the school. When Sammie parents dropped us back off to the school I felt a little like myself again, and I was happy because I missed this person. When I turned around I seen John and Jason heading in our direction, and my world shattered. When Jason asked me why I haven't been returning his calls, I just panicked and ran. Sammie and I got into an argument about what was going on with me but I couldn't tell her so I just got angry with her. I promise I was not mad at her, I was just scared. Later that night I got a text from him and he was so angry. He told me that I had misbehaved and I was going to pay for it, and I was so tired of the abuse. I was tired of the anger and humiliation, and I cannot do it anymore. Everyone is better off without me! I am so bitter and there is no hope for me anymore. I give up.

I kept flipping the pages to see what else she wrote but it was all blank! I started crying and I threw her journal. I felt so angry and I did not understand how I did not know the pain my best friend was going through. I began to blame myself for being so wrapped in my life and with a guy. I started to get mad at John and I questioned if he knew because he used to always tell me to stay out of other people's business. If he knew and didn't say anything I swear I would let the world know that he was a coward. I started thinking what if he was one of the guys who participated in raping her. I punched the wall and I started crying and I just fell to the ground. "Why didn't I know…why…why…?" I felt so extremely guilty and there was nothing I could do because she was gone. I could not run into our dorm and wrap my arms around her and tell her that everything is going to be okay and that we will get through it together. I was too late and she was gone forever. I cried for what felt like hours and God whispered something in my ear and told me to fight. I picked myself up off of the floor and pulled out my computer and started researching how to get justice for rape victims.

Chapter 10-The Untold Secrets

The very next morning I went into my RA's room and asked her if someone was raped who would I report the incident to, and she told me that I would report the incident to the dean. I tried to leave out of her room but she stopped me and asked who was raped, and I told her Erica. Her eyes and mouth dropped open and she asked me how I knew this happened, and I told him that it was all in her journal. Before she could ask me anymore questions I told her that I had to go and report this. I texted John on the way to the dean's office and told him that we needed to talk, and he said he would meet me at the dean's office. When I arrived to the dean's office the secretary asked me what did I want to speak with the dean about and I told her that I wanted to report a serious crime and that because of the crime Erica Harris killed herself. Her eyes widened and she told me to have a seat and that the dean would be with me in a few moments. I swear it felt like I was waiting for hours before the dean invited me into his office, and he had a smirk on his face. He was not too welcoming, and to be honest, he seemed a little creepy.

"Ms. Jones, you said that you have a crime to report that can help us figure out why Ms. Harris committed suicide?" he said.

I was sweating and really nervous but I wanted everyone to know what Jason did to Erica and he deserved to go to jail! "Yes, Erica was raped numerous of times by Jason and some of his friends, and she was scared for her life. She felt that she had no way out, and she became very depressed overtime" I told him.

He looked puzzled and he took a few seconds to collect his thoughts before responding to my allegations. "Are you talking about Jason McGee or another Jason?" he asked. I told him Jason McGee, and that I had evidence of the rape. He tugged on his tie and scratched his head, and he told me to show him what evidence I had. I had made copies of the journal entries and hid the journal in a safe place because I was not too sure that I could trust anyone. He read the entries and his face did not change at all, and I found that very odd because her journal entries were very detailed and it was very cruel what she had went through. Any human being who would read what she went through would have had not been able to keep a straight face. After what it seemed like hours he put the papers down and told me that he is sorry for the loss of my friend. He said she was a wonderful student and that her family means a lot to the school, and he went on to say that he was going to do a full investigation of what happened between the two. I asked if they were going to get the police involved and arrest him and he told me at the time he could not disclose what the school was going to do, but just know that they are going to resolve the situation. He talked so smoothly, quickly, and firmly that I was out of his office before I knew it. I quickly realized, I did not have any answers that I went there for. I told myself that I would give the dean a couple of days before demanding that something be done about what happened to Erica.

When I walked out of the building John was sitting on a bench waiting for me to come out. He tried to give me a hug but I pushed him away and asked him did he know what happened between Erica and Jason. He looked confused and he told me that he did not know what I was talking about, and that he only knew what Jason had told both us that night. I told him that he raped her, tormented her, abused her, and had his friend's gang rape her. He jumped up and told me that he had no idea and that he had nothing to do with Jason and his activities. I looked him in his eyes to see if he was lying to me but he seemed to be telling the truth. I asked him how I knew if he was telling the truth and not lying to me, and he told me because he does not get off shaming women and that he was not going to do anything that was going to put him in jail. He asked me how I knew she was raped and I told him that I found her journal. We stood in silence for a few moments before I told him that we had to get justice for her and asked if he could help me. He told me that he did not know and it was hard for him to believe that Jason was capable of doing something like that. I became very angry that I started yelling at him and told him that she would not lie about something like that. I told him her behavior made sense and that if he asked Jason about that night he would get upset and come up with a lie to explain what happened between them. John just shook his head and told me that he could not see me anymore because I had a lot of drama going on and he told me to go home for a while so I could get over the death of Erica. As he walked away I was angry because he did not believe me, but I was not going to let him stop me from getting justice for her.

I called Erica's father and told him about everything I read in her journal and he became angry. I told him about Jason and how he was the son of the man who was running against him and he said the named sounded familiar, and that he would be coming up to the school to pick me up so we could discuss this in person and not over the phone. I told him okay and that I would bring a copy of her journal with me and he said that was fine. A couple of hours went by and Mr. Harris came to pick me up and we went to a burger restaurant not too far from the school. I gave him the copies of her journal entry and the looks in his eyes as he read them broke my heart. His eyes became filled with tears and he seemed so filled of guilt and anger, and I felt compelled to tell him that it was not his fault. I assured him that Erica became a private person over the last couple of months and she did not tell anyone what happened. He raised his voice and told me that he was her father and that he should have had been there for her and that he was too hard on her. I told Mr. Harris that no one is to blame for her death but Jason, and that sometimes people are so scared of the unknown that they bottle up everything because they feel no one would understand them. I like to believe my words helped Mr. Harris because he seemed to ease up on the papers I gave him. I also told him that I went to the dean's office today and gave him a copy of the journal entries of what happened and he told me he was going to look into it and get back to me. He looked relieved but he told me that we would give them to the end of this week to bring charges against Jason and if they don't then we would take matters into our own hands. I asked him why they would not do anything about what happened to Erica and he told me that sometimes schools like Harrington University try to hide crimes that happens at their schools because they do not want negative attention on their school. I told Mr. Harris that I would let him know what they say and he assured me that we were going to get justice for his daughter. I felt relieved that I had someone helping me get justice for Erica, and it gave me more confidence and strength in talking about rape and suicide on campus.

It was Monday morning and I had not heard anything back from the school board about their plans about prosecuting Jason. I went back to the dean's office and asked to speak to the dean, and this time around the secretary was not so welcoming. She had an attitude and I could not figure out what I did to her, and I started to wonder if she was upset that I was trying to get justice for Erica. I would think that if they had a friend that dealt with a similar situation like mine they would want to get justice for them, but then Mr. Harris words went through my mind and it all made sense. When the dean came into the waiting room he invited me into his office and asked me how my weekend was. I told him it went well and I was only here to see if they are going to go forward with bringing charges against Jason. He told me that they looked into and the board of trustees decided to suspend Jason from all club and school activities for the remainder of the year. I told him that he was graduating this semester and that I did not see how suspending someone from campus activities was a fair punishment. I reminded him that Erica was raped and that she killed herself because of the constant harassment from Jason, and he told me that the school took the journal into consideration but with no actual witnesses they cannot take the words written in the journal. He went on to say that without Erica being here there was no way to actual prove what happened, and to his knowledge I could have had wrote that myself or she could have been mad that he did not call her anymore. He told me that cases like these happen every day with young women becoming upset about hooking up with a guy and when the guy does not call back they state that they have been raped when in reality they have not. I could not believe my ears, and I could not believe that the dean is justifying Jason's behavior. Before I could get another sentence out the dean told me to have a good day and that they had counselors that could help me get through this tough time in my life.

I walked back to my dorm and I was really upset. When I got to my dorm I called Mr. Harris and told him what the dean had said and he became very angry, and he told me that we were going to have to get justice for her by ourselves. We came up with a plan to raise awareness about rape and suicide on campus and how schools try to cover it up. We also decided to make copies of Erica's journal entries and tell people about what she had to go through while on campus and how the school refused to do anything about it. I started making posters and posting things up around the school, and I started passing flyers around the campus about how to speak up about rape. I created chants that said "HEY, HEY, HO, HO, SHE SAID NO AND YOU SAID YES." Before I knew it I started to attract crowds of women of different ethnicities, and they were helping me get Erica's story out there. The school tried to threaten us and tell us that we were having a violent protest and that if we did not stop we were going to get expelled from the school. I did not care and neither did the other protestors and we continue to protest day and night telling people about what happened to Erica, and how the school refused to do anything. One day I ran into Jason while passing out flyers and he was so angry.

"Why are you doing this to me? I cannot go anywhere without people staring at me and blaming me for Erica's death and calling me a rapist!" he said.

"Did you think of the pain you caused Erica? Did you stop when she told you to stop? No you didn't! You continued to rape her over and over, and it is because of you she is no longer here!" I yelled. As we were yelling at one another, people started coming over and chanting "HEY HEY HO HO SHE SAID NO AND YOU SAID YES!" He turned around and walked away really fast and covered up his face. It was that moment that I was so proud of myself and I felt Erica's presence. I knew if she was still here she would be very proud of me. As I was in my thoughts, John came over to me and apologized for his behavior and his reaction to what I told him. I told him that it was okay and that I understood that sometimes we think we know somebody when in reality we don't. I handed him a poster and gave him a kiss and we started walking around the school with the rest of the protestors and we were chanting "HEY HEY HO HO SHE SAID NO AND YOU SAID YES!"

The next morning Mr. Harris came up to the school and he had Fox 5 with him, and I was so happy and I started crying. He came over to me and he gave me a hug and thanked me for everything that I have done for his daughter and that this would of never had happened without me. He started crying and I told him that this is only the beginning and that I loved her like she was my own sister and I am not stopping until she gets justice. He grabbed my hand and brought me in the direction of the reporters and they asked me what was going on at the school, and I told them. It was November 2014 when Erica and I went over to Jason McGee and Johnathan Jefferson apartment to watch movies and to hang out, and that is where Jason raped and abused Erica Harris for hours. He blackmailed her, raped her repeatedly, and allowed his friends to rape her for the last past couple months. She told him no several times and he ignored her and told her yes and that he owned her. Jason is a coward, and a boy who needs to be little women to get off, and when I brought this to the schools attention they blamed Erica! They suspended Jason from all school activities for the remainder of Jason's last semester and told me get counseling. Rape and suicide on campus is real and we will not stop until Erica receives justice. After I finished talking, the reporter looked back at the camera and gave her closing speech. When they were done recording she told me that I was brave and that it was a good thing that I was getting justice for my friend. I gave her a hug and I thanked her for coming to the school and helping me get her story out and she said it was no problem and that people need to know what goes on at universities like these before letting their children come to them.

The reporter and her crew started taking other people's statements and what they thought about the situation and how they knew Erica. I sat down on a bench and I just took a moment to look around and I started to smile because I found the courage to help my friend after all. As I sat and reminisced about Erica and I, a young woman came up to me and thanked me for coming forward and getting justice for Erica. I told her that Erica was an amazing person and that she did not deserve what Jason did to her. She went on to tell me that when she was a freshmen last year and she went to a party that Jason was having. They were drinking and having a good time, and she felt dizzy and when she regained consciousness, he had her tied up and he was forcing himself into her. She started crying and telling me the pain he put her through, and it was because I stood up to him and told everyone what he did to Erica that she could tell people what he did to her. I gave her a hug and I told her that we would get justice for what he has done to Erica and for what he has done to her. I brought her over to where the reporter and Mr. Harris was and I told the reporter that she was also another rape victim and that Jason was the person who raped her. The reporter asked her if she wanted to tell everyone what had happened to her and she looked at me and told her yes. I held her hand as she told the reporter what happened to her and how the school refused to help her.

Later that night I decided to have a candle light vigil for Erica and to my surprise the entire circle in front of the school was filled with a lot of people. My parents were there and so were Mr. and Mrs. Harris, and it brought tears to my eyes and I took a deep breath before I started speaking to everyone. Erica was a very beautiful person inside and out and everyone who knew her loved her. From the very first time I met her she was so full of life and she always smiled and laughed at everything. She used to say that we were going to have a blast this year and that we had so much to explore and I never thought that I would had to say goodbye to her so soon. I blamed myself for her death because I felt that as a friend you should always know what is going on with your friends, and that there would be no secretes between one another but sometimes that isn't the case. As human beings we become so busy with our lives that we tend to forget about the people that means the most to us, and I ignored all of the signs that something was wrong with my friend. That is probably something I am going to blame myself for the rest of my life for but I will not blame myself for being a bad friend. I was a wonderful friend to her and she was an amazing friend to me. We had a bond that was unexplainable and it was because of her that I found out who I really was, and I am so grateful for her. She taught me to love myself no matter what and to be okay with whom I am, and I am going to miss her dearly. I want tonight to be about her and all of the amazing things she has done in her life. On tonight we light a candle in her memory and we remember all of the good times we each shared with her.

We all lite our candles and her parents got in front of everyone and told everyone about their daughter and how they missed her and how amazing she was. I looked into the crowd and my mother mouthed that she was so proud of me and I blew a kiss to her. We sat in silence and we all let the candles light until they burned out the next morning. I sat down on a bench that Erica and I used to sit on all of the time and I reminisced on everything we talked about and all of the fun adventures we went on. I did not cry this time instead, I smiled and closed my eyes. I imagined that I was sitting and talking to her about my plans over the summer and how I was going to come visit her. I imagined that she was smiling at me and that she was laughing, and it was at that moment that I knew she was no longer in pain. The next morning one of the women from the protest ran into my dorm and told me to go outside. I threw on some sweat pants and a t-shirt and some gym shoes. When I got outside I saw the police escorting Jason to the police car in handcuffs and the look on his face was priceless. He thought he would never get caught, and he probably would have, if I had dropped it. I started smiling and I just listened to everyone chanting "HEY HEY HO HO SHE SAID NO AND YOU SAID YES!" I knew this was just the beginning but I was willing to see this thing through.

Chapter 11-Goodbye

It was June and the trial was very long. It went on for about three months and I like to believe because of his father. During the trial there were about three other women that came forward about Jason assaulting them and they each said that he raped them more than once. They were all different ethnicities and they all were very pretty. I thought he had something against black women but it turned out he had something against all women. Jason was found guilty on all counts of rape against Erica and for the rape of the other women, and he was serving the maximum of thirty years in prison with the possibility of parole. The guys that ganged raped Erica were charged and they were serving fifteen years in prison with the possibility of parole. Harrington University was fined $300,000 for covering up rape allegations and failing to act or report them to the police officials. The women who were raped thanked me for standing up to Jason and for helping them get justice. I assured them that I could have had not done it without them, and I gave them a hug and walked over to Mr. Harris. Both Mr. and Mrs. Harris gave me a hug and thanked me for all of my help and they told my parents that they have done a wonderful job raising a brave woman. They went on to say that I am welcomed to come visit them anytime and they would like for us all to keep in contact and I told them I would. I asked Mr. Harris if he was going to be the new judge of family court in Texas, and he told me that he was going to be the new judge in the criminal's court and I told him congratulations and he thanked me.

When I got through with talking and shaking everyone's hand I noticed that John was standing around waiting for me. I went over to him and I thanked him for being supportive over these past months and that I appreciated his help and his words of encouragement. He told me it was not a problem at all. He went on to tell me about how what I did was an amazing thing and that he was proud of me. I gave him a hug and asked him if he wanted to meet my parents, and he said yeah. My parents and John seemed to connect right away and I was finally in a good place. We all went back to my house to have dinner and I wanted John to meet my little sister Kate. John and I were watching television and we started kissing and he pulled back and told me that he wanted to ask me something. I told him that he could ask me anything, and he told me that he really cared about me and that although he was officially done with school and I was still in school he wanted me to be his girlfriend. I was so excited and I told him of course I would be his girlfriend. He pulled out a bracelet out of his pocket and he put it on my arm and gave me a kiss. We continued watching movies and we were laughing and joking about our plans over the summer.

John and I decided to drive to Texas to go visit Erica at her grave and I was really excited. When we arrived to her grave I began to cry and John just held my hand and told me that everything was going to be okay. I started talking to Erica's grave, "Hey Erica, I really miss you and I wish you could be here with me right now, but I know you are in a better place now. Jason received thirty years in prison and the other guys got what they deserved as well. It is going to be hard to go back to Harrington University without you but I know that you would want me to keep going. I brought my grades up and I am officially apart of the journalism club and I started a rape and suicide group at school so other people would not have to go through what you did alone. I will never forget you or the bond we shared, and I remember the promises we made to one another. I will forever keep them in my heart. I love you girly!" I just sat and stared at her grave with John. I cried and I laughed. I told her this was not goodbye but it was a see you later and we walked back to the car. That summer John and I became very close and I continued to raise awareness about rape and suicide on campus.

■ ■

Although, this was a fictional story, rape does happen on college campus and it is not to be taken lightly. 1 in 4 women in college has been the victim of rape and 90% of them know their rapist. 60% of male college students admitted to committing some form of rape. Every 21 hours there is another rape on an American college campus. 90% of rape happens under the influence of alcohol (crisisconnectioninic.org). 33% of rape victims have suicidal thoughts. 13% of rape victims will attempt suicide (suicide.org). We need to stand together and prevent rape from happening on our campuses!

As humans we tend to get distracted with material things and our everyday lives that we tend to ignore our loved ones. Everyone around you is going through something and it only takes a second to ask them what is going on with them or how have they been. If someone does not want to be bothered or they do not want to tell you right away what is going on with them, which is okay. We just have to have patience with them and understand that depending on what people are going through it takes time for people to open up. We have to let people know that we love and we care about them, and just by giving someone a hug can go a long way. Rape and suicide is very serious and we need to make a stand today. "This is real! We lose too many lives or self-esteems because we are too busy to check in."

About the Author

I was born in the spring of 1993, in Southfield, MI. Both of my parents are well educated, and I'm the only girl of five brothers. I was raised to believe I could do anything I set my mind to. I always had a passion for writing, it is the way I made sense of the world around me, and the challenges people face of a daily basics. As a under graduate, I took a creative writing class, and it allowed me to explore my imagination and how I could create a story that could allow people to think outside of the box.

I graduated from Oakland University with honors in May of 2015 with a Bachelor of Arts degree in communication. I am a strong believer of Christ and that I can do all things through God that strengthens me. Every poem or book I write, I hope to open the minds and hearts of my audience, in the hopes that we can come together to make the world a better place.